PUFFIN BOOKS

Aussie Bites

Rattler's Place

When Guy moves to his new house,
things are not quite right. There's no
bike, no skateboard, and worst of all
there's no Digby, the dog.

But then there is Rattler, and
suddenly things are not so bad,
after all . . .

Puffin Books

Published by the Penguin Group
Penguin Books Australia Ltd
250 Camberwell Road,
Camberwell, Victoria 3124, Australia
Penguin Books Ltd
80 Strand, London WC2R 0RL, England
Penguin Putnam Inc.
375 Hudson Street, New York, New York 10014, USA
Penguin Books, a division of Pearson Canada
10 Alcorn Avenue, Toronto, Ontario, Canada M4V 3B2
Penguin Books (N.Z.) Ltd
Cnr Rosedale and Airborne Roads, Albany, Auckland, New Zealand
Penguin Books (South Africa) (Pty) Ltd
24 Sturdee Avenue, Rosebank, Johannesburg 2196, South Africa
Penguin Books India (P) Ltd
11, Community Centre, Panchsheel Park, New Delhi 110 017, India

Rattler's Place first published by Penguin Books Australia, 1997
The Sugar Gum Tree first published by Penguin Books Australia
in Viking, 1991 and in Puffin, 1993
The Water-Dragons first published by Penguin Books Australia, 1999
This combined edition first published by Penguin Books Australia, 2002

3 5 7 9 10 8 6 4 2

Typeset in New Century School Book by Post Pre-press Group, Brisbane, Queensland
Printed and bound in Australia by McPherson's Printing Group, Maryborough, Victoria

Series designed by Ruth Grüner
Series editor: Kay Ronai

National Library of Australia
Cataloguing-in-Publication data:

Wrightson, Patricia, 1921- .
Great Aussie bites.

ISBN 0 7343 0490 0.

1. Moving, Household - Juvenile fiction. 2. Girls -
Juvenile fiction. 3. Water-dragons - Juvenile fiction. I.
Cox, David, 1933- . II. Wrightson, Patricia, 1921- Water
dragons. III. Wrightson, Patricia, 1921- Rattler's place.
IV. Wrightson, Patricia, 1921- Sugar-gum tree. V. Title.
(Series : Aussie bites).

A823.3

www.puffin.com.au

Aussie Bites

Rattler's Place

Patricia Wrightson

Illustrated by David Cox

Puffin Books

ONE

It was an old house, but the Dents had just bought it, so it was new for them: a long way from their old home. The town was new for them too. Guy thought he would like living here when school started. There would be people then, and things to do.

Now it was lonely. There was no one next door because the house was a little way out of town. Dad was away all day, looking for a shop to buy. Mum

was doing stuff on the computer
and fixing the house. Katie was
too little for Guy's games.

He helped Mum a bit with the
house. The beds and tables and
chairs were in the right places,
but they still didn't look right.
Some pretty important things
hadn't even come yet: Guy's
skateboard and football; Katie's
doll and its stuff, and a lot of
her old rag animals;
the building sets
and train set
and bikes . . . All
their special things,
as well as Digby their dog.

In the house a lot of cupboards and shelves were still empty, because there were boxes still full. You opened up a box and found towels or sheets or books;

then you had to put them away in the new place. Guy and Mum were doing that now. Mum had blankets in her box, and Guy had a lot of old, clean dusters.

'Sort them into small and big ones, will you, Guy?'

Guy started two piles. 'Will Digby be all right?' he asked. 'When will he get here?'

Mum had answered these questions pretty often, but she knew Guy was worried so she answered them again. 'He's safe in the Dog's Home till that flood goes down. He'll come with your bikes and things; we don't know when, but it won't be long.'

'He'll like it here,' said Guy. 'That big back yard going down the hill, and the bush outside the fence.'

'And us being here,' said Mum, and they smiled.

Katie came in. She was nursing a brick. She had found it in the garage and carried it all the way up the back stairs.

'Oh Katie!' cried Mum. 'A dirty old brick?'

Katie looked surprised. 'It's not dirty. It's Elly. Will you dress her, Mum?'

'But she's so heavy, Kate. If she

falls on your foot she might break
your toe.'

Katie screwed up her eyes,
trying to find the right words.
'Babies have to be heavy,' she said
at last.

Mum sighed. 'They have to be
bathed, too. I'll give you a dish of
water and some soap, and Guy
will give you that old towel he's
found. And is this a good frock for

Elly?' She took out of Guy's box an old, white curtain with lace on it, and Katie reached for it. 'Come on, then,' said Mum. 'I think there's some baby powder you can use.'

They went away to the bathroom. Guy kept on sorting the dusters till Mum came back. 'I'll *buy* her a doll in a day or so,' Mum fretted, 'if only I can get to the shops.'

'It's all right,' said Guy. 'She likes the brick.'

Soon they had emptied their boxes and put the things away in cupboards. 'Now,' said Mum, 'I have to start the computer and get on with those sums Dad brought home. Will you keep an eye on Katie? I think she's outside again. You could take her a little way into the scrub if you liked.'

'Not with the brick,' said Guy. 'And she won't go without it. I'll wait for Digby. *He'll* like the scrub.'

He went out through the kitchen, across the back verandah, to the landing where the back stairs went down. Even though the front steps were low, these were high because of the steep hill.

Under the high verandah was a paved place for wet days, or for Digby to sleep. At one end of it was the laundry, at the other the garage. Katie might be there, looking for another doll . . . But suddenly there was a loud *crash!* in the house.

Brick! Bathroom! Tiles! Guy turned and rushed upstairs. So

far no one was yelling; he stopped rushing and went through the kitchen to listen.

'She didn't hurt herself,' Katie was saying stiffly. 'It's a rubber mat.'

'She didn't break the tiles, either,' said Mum, just as stiffly. 'But bathrooms are dangerous. Take her downstairs.'

Guy went back down. His mind was saying *what was it? what was it?* but not about the crash. He thought that with the crash had come another sound: a quiet ringing, like a tiny bell.

TWO

Katie made a bed for Elly in an empty box. She dressed Elly in the white curtain and snuggled her in the old towel. She fed her and washed her and took her for walks. 'You're growing so big,' she sighed, sitting down because the brick was heavy.

Mum said, 'I wish that flood would go down. I'll ring the carriers again.' She sounded as if it were her fault that Katie was playing with a brick.

'Will I paint a face on her for you?' Dad asked Katie. She stared at him for some time.

'Asleep or awake?' she asked at last.

Dad looked puzzled. 'Which do you want?'

'Both,' said Katie. 'And sometimes she cries.'

Dad went off looking helpless. Guy decided he would never have children; you had to worry too much. As far as he could see, Katie was happy with Elly while she waited for her own doll, and what was wrong with that? He only wished he could use a brick for a skateboard.

He couldn't unpack boxes if Mum was too busy to say where things should go. He couldn't settle down to read while everything felt so new. He went into the bush once or twice, and that wasn't bad.

There was a creek at the bottom of the hill. A pipe came out under the Dents' back fence into a steep little gully; that must be to take away water from their place. The little gully ran down into the creek. There was no water running just now, but the creek had pools with frogs' eggs and skaters and water-spiders.

He prowled about the house, too, getting to know it better. The space underneath was dark and secret: low in front and high at the back, all walled in by bricks. Guy thought there must be a way for workmen to get in: there could

be water-pipes and electric wires to fix. But he couldn't find a way in.

The garage joined on to that high, blank wall. In a corner bricks were stacked into a tall pillar. You could build a racing car with those; or when school started, other boys might help Guy think of better things to build.

He checked the garden. There wasn't much; just some roses and ferns out the front, where it wasn't so steep. Stuff had been planted out the back, but most of it was gone. The steep yard looked a bit humpy with its thick, long grass.

In the middle of the back fence there were still some battered old shrubs and vines. Behind them, someone had written in pencil on the brown paint of the fence.

The scrawled, faded old letters were hard to read, but Guy made them out at last: RATTLER'S PLACE.

That felt funny. It was like

something going on that you
didn't know about, or having a
ghost peep over your shoulder.
Who was Rattler? Why was this
his place? What did he do here in
Guy's own yard?

Guy looked all along the fence

to see if anyone from long ago
had written anything else.
Tomorrow he'd look on the other
fences. And on the garage walls.
And underneath the back stairs,
and any hidden places.

That night, at dinner, Dad said,
'Better cover your ears up
tomorrow. They're going to blow
up that old tower in town.'

'The old mill?' cried Guy. 'Will it
come down in one shot?'

'I should think so.'

'Do we have to cover up our
ears all day?' asked Katie.

'Only till ten o'clock,' said Dad,
and Mum smiled.

Guy snorted. 'We won't even hear it.' He turned to his parents. 'Can I go and watch?'

Mum looked unhappy. 'It ought to be yes, you're so sensible. But I'd be nervous. If you just had a mate, so you could watch out for each other . . .

As soon as school starts you can watch towers being blown up.'

'But see me first,' said Dad. 'And Katie's ears are safe enough, but still I think you'll hear it tomorrow.'

Guy had forgotten the tower when he heard the blast next day. It was a big noise, deep and rumbling. He was sitting on the back stairs, and he felt them shake. A gust of wind brushed over the scrub. From somewhere near came a faint, clear *tang!* like a very small bell.

'What *is* it?' Guy muttered, and went to look in the laundry. The taps were metal, but they didn't go *tang!* if you banged them or shook them. Neither did the electric iron, or the windows, or the trolley for wheeling out the clothes.

He went into the garage. Dad had taken the car. There were nails and screws in jars, and tools on a bench and the mower in a corner. None of them went *tang!* whatever he did. There were empty boxes, waiting for the others that were still in the house. There was a big basket for Digby, when he came. Guy thought there were enough things to think about without a *tang!* He put Digby's

basket out near the stairs and
went off to look for writings on
fences.

He found one quite soon. It was just at the corner, where the side fence joined the back one. An old, worn-out daisy bush nearly hid it. The writing, in pencil, said R.I.P. BRENDA, and there was an arrow pointing down. Guy felt a bit creepy, but that was crazy. He got the spade from the garage and started to dig.

He had to move aside branches and silver-green daisy leaves. The ground was dry and hard, but he kept chopping it with the spade. Soon he could see something pink and shiny: at least Brenda hadn't been a cat. He crouched down to

work with his hands, and
uncovered a pink, shiny doll,
badly dented and all in bits. Its
legs and arms and head had come
off, and old, grey elastic straggled
from them.

This was not Guy's scene. He
went to find Katie.

THREE

'She's all broken,' said Katie.

'I could fix her,' said Guy.

'Her face is all squashed.'

'I could do it like panel-beating.'

'No,' said Katie. 'Cover her up. I'll put flowers there.'

She went away, breathing heavily from the weight of Elly. They left behind them the smell of baby powder.

Guy scraped the soil over the bits of pink doll and took the

spade back to the garage. It wasn't
fair that Katie should have both
Elly and a grave to put flowers on,
while he couldn't find Rattler or
even the *tang!*

He had another look at Rattler's
Place: there was no arrow and no
R.I.P. The roots of the bushes and
shrubs bulged up from the ground
where the pipe went through into
the gully; you couldn't dig a hole
there, even if it said R.I.P. He
went off to look for writing on the
walls of the garage.

It had only two proper walls; its
front one was a big roller-door,
and its side joined onto the house.

There was no writing. He went
inside and turned on the light.

The side wall was really part
of the brick wall that went all
round the house and hid the
space underneath. Guy couldn't
see quite all of it, because of the
stack of bricks. He went closer.
There was too much shadow. He
pushed the bricks a little bit, not
meaning to.

The stack swayed – bulged –
Guy dived under a bench. The
bricks came down with a crashing
and grinding. The roller-door
rattled and shook. And there
came a *tang!* like a small bell.

Guy hardly heard it. The bricks
were all over the floor, he would
have to clear them up before Dad
brought the car in. There would
have to be two stacks,
because he couldn't
reach high
enough for one …

Then his skin
felt the air
moving.

His nose caught a stale, stuffy smell. His ears remembered a *tang!* Something had changed, something was different. He forgot the bricks and began to look.

He found it at once: a dark doorway into the secret, hidden space under the house. There was no door. The bricks, stacked

in front of it, had hidden the opening. The slow-moving air came from it; and the stale smell; and perhaps the small bell-sound?

Guy crept through the hole. He stayed near it in case something else might fall on him. All the secret space was dark as night, but a little bit of light came in from the garage. Not far inside the opening there was a small, bright flicker. Guy stared at it, and the tiny, bright flicker shone back.

After a time, Guy's eyes began to see more in the dark. There was a dull silvery shape around the flicker. There were wheels.

He moved forward into the dark,
touching and feeling. Two wheels
at the back . . . a bigger one in
front . . . some sort of trike.

No handlebars! And the pedals
wouldn't move . . . A head, it had
a head! It wasn't a trike now.
Someone had made it into
something else! Guy dragged it
through the hole into the garage.
It had an ugly, fierce, wooden

head with leather ears, a bit like a horse.

The head was fixed to the stem where the trike's handlebars should join on. Nailed to its wooden neck were leather reins to hold on by, and round the stem was a wire ring with a piece of tin hanging from it. The tin, dangling on the wire, made a sound like *tang!*

And painted on it in rather wobbly
letters was a name: RATTLER.

Guy gazed in delight. So this
was Rattler! He had a Place down
at the back fence. You could ride
him; there was a rusty seat with
no padding. But you couldn't
make him go; the pedals
wouldn't work. You
would have to let
him run down the
hill and then
push him
back up.

You couldn't steer, so he could run anywhere he liked; and you couldn't hang on except with the grotty old reins. It might take a while learning to ride him, and it might be fun.

He wheeled Rattler out through the side door of the garage, near the stairs. He still had all those bricks to stack up. Should he block up the old doorway again? It might be good to park the bikes just inside it. Or it might be better having a dark, secret place under the house for hiding things; look how well it had hidden Rattler.

He left that for Dad to say,

and stacked the bricks over the hole. Guy's stack was twice as wide and half as high as the old one. He was just finishing it when he heard Katie's voice.

'I'm riding my horse, Elly. You watch, you're too little.'

'No!' shouted Guy, and ran out of the garage. Elly squatted on the stairs in its white curtain, square and safe like a brick. Katie stood looking at Rattler.

Guy got there fast. He flung himself on Rattler's rusty seat and sat as hard as he could. 'He's *not* yours, Katie, he's mine. I found him and you don't even know his name.'

'It's Silver,' said Katie at once,
looking at the trike.

'It's not, see? It's written here.
It's Rattler, and you can't ride him.'

'I can so!'

'Not unless Mum says. He's
dangerous. You could have a
nasty fall.'

'Go on, then,' said Katie, not believing him. 'You show.'

Guy settled himself behind the big front wheel and took the reins. With his feet on the ground, he walked Rattler out of the paved place to the steep slope of the hill. He was fizzing inside, looking down at Rattler's Place: he was going to crash into those bushes, and probably the fence. He might even break a leg. He gave a push and put his feet quickly up on the pedals.

Rattler rolled forward, not too fast but bouncing a bit. At once he got faster, rattling and swaying a lot. Then his wheels were singing, he rocked from side to side, the fence was rushing up, and Guy cried, 'Zeeeee!' They crashed into the fence and were tossed among the battered bushes of Rattler's Place.

FOUR

Guy lay panting for a moment.
He could hear Katie's squeals of
fright and laughter up near the
house. It didn't sound as if she
wanted a ride. Carefully he lifted
himself and Rattler out of the
bushes.

It was funny, but he wasn't hurt at all. Maybe the big front wheel and Rattler's great wooden head had done all the crashing. And the bushes must help; that could be why this was Rattler's Place. He began the job of pushing Rattler back up the hill.

He went sloping across it to make the hill less steep, pulling Rattler behind him by the back axle. They were nearly at the top, and right over near the side fence, when he stopped for a rest. He let go the wheels to rub his sore hands. Before he knew it, Rattler had started a backwards

run down the hill.

Guy stood and watched. This
time there must be a crash into
the fence; he would see it happen
. . . But it didn't happen. First
Rattler started his run down
the hill, then he swung across it.
He lurched sideways and down,
picking up speed. At last he went

swooping down and crashed into the bushes at the same place as before. Guy had to go down and bring him up again.

This time he tried from the garage. Katie sat on the stairs and watched. Rattler started off going straight down the hill, lurched and swung aside, picked up speed and hurtled down into the bushes again.

Guy started another run from a different place. He tried from four more places. Sometimes he rode Rattler, sometimes he just stood and watched. Every time, whatever he did, Rattler swung round towards his own place and ran into it.

'No wonder they wrote it on the fence,' Guy thought. It was beginning to bother him. He let Rattler run down again into the bushes and stay there. He didn't think Katie would drag the old horse up from there, and he didn't want her riding it. He wasn't going to be blamed for a bleeding, broken Katie.

He went inside to find Mum. She was working at the computer again. 'There's this kind of a trike,' said Guy. 'Only it works like a billycart.' He spoke slowly

and loudly, watching her face to
see if she heard. You had to do
that when Mum was thinking.
'I found it under the house,' he

said, still slowly. 'It goes fast
down the back yard, but it
crosses over too. IT ALWAYS
GOES TO THE SAME PLACE.'

Mum's head jerked towards him for a moment. 'Hmm?' she said.

'Every single time. Starting anywhere.'

'It's the hill,' said Mum vaguely. She turned back to the computer. 'Don't let Kate fall off.'

'All right,' sighed Guy, and went slowly away. He would have to wait till Dad came home. He might as well have another look at Rattler and maybe a good look under the house. There ought to be a torch somewhere . . .

He remembered the torch was in the car. He wasn't going into that darkness till he could see what was there, so he had some more rides on Rattler. Then he went stamping about the steep back yard looking for wires, or tracks, or something hidden in the grass; something that would make Rattler run across the yard as well as down, and always crash into the same place. He still hadn't found anything when Dad came home.

Dad was a lot more interested than Mum had been, probably because he wasn't tied up with the computer. He said things the way he did when he was joining in, like 'bottler!' when he saw Rattler and 'hooly-dooly!' when Guy showed

him the useless pedals and the old
reins. But when he saw how every
ride ended at Rattler's Place he
looked pleased, and went prowling
through the grass as Guy had
done. And at last he said, 'Drains.'

'No!' cried Guy. 'You'd trip in

them and feel them! And the front wheel would stomp down into them!'

'You can feel them when you know,' said Dad. 'Spoon drains: wide and shallow, so you can mow across them. There's one down the middle of the yard and one on each side, like a big fan going to that drainpipe at the bottom. So wherever Rattler starts, he's got to run into one of the drains. Then he just stays in it till he gets to the fence. When I mow the grass you'll see.'

So then Guy showed Dad the bricks, fallen over and piled up

again; and behind them the secret place where Rattler had been hidden, making his tiny, ringing noises in the dark.

'There's a lot of room, isn't there? Will we keep our bikes in there, do you reckon?'

'Maybe,' said Dad. 'We'll see. It mightn't be easy getting them in and out, and they aren't even here yet.'

'Besides,' said Guy, 'it's a whopping big place. You could do things with it. You could make a museum, or keep frogs.' He was thinking of the creek down in the gully, and the tadpoles.

FIVE

The bikes came the very next day. A small, shabby truck came rumbling along the road and stopped outside the house. There, on its tray, were the bikes; and the big wooden crate that had all Guy's and Katie's special things in it; and most of all, in another big crate, there was Digby.

While the truck was still in town, his nose had been telling him that the Dent family, and

their carpets and chairs and
other things, were somewhere
near. He was a big, black and tan
dog, leaping about inside his
crate, barking with joy and
excitement.

Mum and Guy and Katie
rushed out, and the truck's driver
seemed glad to see them. 'Digby!'
they shouted, and Guy climbed

up on the truck. Digby's crate had a door with a wire hook. Guy tugged at the hook, and Digby exploded out of it.

He leapt at Guy and knocked him over. He jumped down to the road and knocked Katie over. Then he threw himself at Mum. She had taken hold of the truck's door and didn't fall over; she managed to give Digby a big hug.

That gave Guy and Katie a chance to hug him too, and soon Digby was quieter. By then, the driver had unloaded the bikes and crate. Mum paid him some money and he drove off quickly.

'I think Digby was a bit too big for him,' said Mum, watching him go.

'Him,' snorted Guy. 'Digby's water was all spilt in the crate. And there were just *two raw eggs* in a saucer.'

'Well,' said Mum, 'it probably wasn't the man's fault. You and Katie take Digby round to his kennel and put a big dish of water there, and I'll find him something to eat. And then, at *last,* you can take your things out of their crate. You can have your skateboard, Guy. And Kate, you'll have Mary again.'

'Mary! Hooray!' shouted Katie, jumping up and down.

They settled Digby in his kennel and he had a long drink of water; but he didn't want to eat. He kept following them around as if they might go away again; or else he lay somewhere close, just watching.

Mum opened the crate in the front yard. 'We won't take everything out yet; only what you want now. Come and look.'

The things in the crate looked older and shabbier than they had before. 'Did they get caught in the flood?' Guy asked.

Mum laughed. 'Of course not.
They look different when you
haven't seen them for a while.

This one looks the same, anyway.'
She lifted out a silky-haired doll
in a frilly dress and white shoes,
and put it into Katie's arms.

Katie gazed at it. The doll stared back with its shiny-blue eyes and smiled its sweet, still smile. Katie said 'Mary' a bit shyly, and rocked the doll up and down once or twice. Then she put it down quickly and ran away.

'What on earth – ?' cried Mum, looking after her.

'She's too excited,' said Guy. 'It doesn't matter. She's got what she wants.' He hooked his ribs over the edge of the crate and leaned in for his skateboard. 'I'll come and take the bikes round the back. Will the rest be all right till Digby's got used to home?' He dropped down from the crate.

Mum sounded a little tired. 'I think so. I'm doing some letters for Dad anyway.'

Guy nodded and tucked his skateboard under his arm. 'I'll take this too. She'll want it,' he said, picking up Mary by one arm as he passed.

Katie was sitting at the bottom of the back stairs, nursing Elly. Guy put Mary down beside her. 'There. Now you can put the heavy old brick back in the garage.'

'Babies *have* to be heavy!' shouted Katie.

'They have to have faces and

arms and legs too, *don't* they?'
shouted Guy.

'They can *change* their faces!
Sometimes they cry! They don't
just keep smiling and staring at
you!'

Guy knew she felt sore, because
he did too; but he didn't really know
why. He said, 'Look, Kate, Mum and
Dad got you the best doll in the

shop for your birthday and you loved it and that's it there. So keep your old brick if you want to; you've got whatever you want. Soon you'll be dressing the doll.'

He went to bring the two bikes round and prop them near the laundry. Katie's looked very small, but that was from not seeing it for a while. His own was still the right size. He put the skateboard there with them, because the road out the front was a bit soft for it, and the back yard a bit too steep.

He was still feeling sore. He remembered Rattler – what would Digby think of Rattler? He'd better

find out. He went to drag it out of
the dark place under the house.

Digby jumped up at once. He
sniffed at Rattler and growled.
Guy started his ride, and Digby
raced behind snapping at the axle

with his teeth. All three together,
they hurtled into the bushes at
Rattler's Place. Guy lay there
while Digby barked angrily and
prodded at Guy with his nose.

They had another go, by another
track. The turning fooled Digby; he
had to chase after Rattler, and he
started prancing and grinning
and leaping in play.
Guy started to laugh.

Soon Digby was wild with excitement and Guy laughed till he ached. They had more runs, and made so much noise that Mum came out to see. Katie watched, nursing both dolls and laughing too.

They were still doing it when Dad came home. Digby saw him first and went bounding up the hill. Guy crawled out from the bushes. 'Hi, Dad!' he shouted. 'Our things came!'

'So I see!' called Dad. He braced himself against the wall just in time. Digby leapt at him.

From Patricia Wrightson

As a child I was one of a family of six, with
two older sisters and three younger brothers.
I grew up in the country areas of the North
Coast of New South Wales and went to a range
of different schools. All of my schools assumed
I would become a writer, but I very nearly
didn't. I was not sure where to begin, was
awed by the great writers and couldn't believe
there was any excuse for trying. Only after
I had been married and divorced and had two
children (Jenny and Peter) did I dare begin by
producing stories for them. I was very lucky to
begin by accident in so demanding a school.

From David Cox

For me, illustrating a book is half work
and half play. The work part comes at the
beginning, when I am working out the
characters: what they look like and, especially,
what they feel. Once I begin to know the
characters well, drawing them is more like
play. The more I like the story, the easier it is
to illustrate. And that is what makes it
pleasant to illustrate a story by Patricia
Wrightson: she writes so very well.

PUFFIN BOOKS

Aussie Bites

The Sugar-Gum Tree

Sarah Bell and Penny May
were best friends. Sometimes they
had fights, but after the fights
they were best friends again.

Then one day they had
a very bad fight.

Aussie Bites

The Sugar-Gum Tree

Patricia Wrightson

Illustrated by David Cox

Puffin Books

One

Sarah Bell and Penny May were
best friends. They both played in
the Bells' yard, or they both played
in the Mays' yard.

Sometimes they had fights.
Then Sarah talked and smiled in a
grown-up way. It made Penny mad.
If she stomped about and shouted
a bit, the fight was soon over; but

1

if Penny had a red face and tight-shut lips, it was a bad fight.

After the fights they were best friends again.

Sarah was making a house,

under the sugar-gum tree in her
back yard. Penny came round
to help. There was a lot of stuff
lying around the tree. Penny
had a good look.

'Where did the rug come from?'
she asked.

'The tip,' Sarah told her. 'When
Dad took me. It's clean, even.
Mum helped me.'

'It's magic. What are the bricks
for?'

'The stove, I think. Or it could
be chairs.'

'There's a lot. You can have

a little stove and two chairs.'

Sarah frowned; she hadn't
made up her mind. She said,
'The stove has to fit the pan
Mum gave me.'

Penny went to look at the pan.
'Cups too!' she cried. 'Your
mother gave you cups!'

'Only two,' said Sarah. 'And
they're cracked.'

'I was going to bring my old
teaset!'

'You still can,' said Sarah

quickly, because she could tell
that Penny was hurt. 'We need
more cups and there's no
teapot.'

'You know my teapot's broken,'
Penny said in a grumpy way.

She *was* hurt.

The house was made from
an old quilt. Sarah tied it to
the tree with string.

'That needs a nail,' said
Penny. She was good with nails.
She went into Mr Bell's shed

and came back with a hammer
and a nail.

'Oh, Penny!' cried Sarah. 'You
can't put a nail in Dad's good
sugar-gum tree.' Sarah was good
with string, and it was her house.

'If a wind comes,' said Penny,
'the whole house could blow
away.' She stood on an apple-
crate and nailed the quilt to
the tree.

'Now you've made the house
crooked,' Sarah told her crossly.

Penny reached up to pull the
quilt straight. There was a loud,
cracking noise, and she tumbled
down. The thin wood of the apple-
crate had broken.

'Look what you've done!' cried Sarah. 'That was my table! Penny May, you're a gloop!'

Penny stood up slowly. She was frowning, and there was a long, red scratch on her leg. She said, 'That's not very nice. Calling people a . . .'

'A gloop,' said Sarah, helping

in a grown-up way.

'. . . when they've fallen down

and hurt their leg and they're

only trying to help. You ought to

say sorry.'

'Me?' said Sarah, smiling her

grown-up
smile. '*You*
ought to say
sorry.
Putting
nails into
Dad's tree
and
breaking my
table. Go on. Say you're sorry.'

Penny shut her lips tight. Her
face went red. She jumped at
a branch of the sugar-gum tree,

pulled herself up and began
to climb.

'Come down!' Sarah called, but
Penny went on climbing. 'You're

only being another gloop!' cried
Sarah.

Penny climbed quite high.
Then she sat in the fork of
a branch and shouted angrily,
'I won't come down till you say
you're sorry!'

Two

Sarah was upset; but of course she wasn't sorry. It was her house, and people should make their house their own way. It wasn't fair for Sarah to say sorry when Penny was the one to blame. But when would Penny come down from the tree?

Sarah didn't know what to do,

so she went on making the
house. Penny went on sitting in
the tree. She didn't even look
down, but stared away over all
the back yards.

Sarah put the old rug into
the house for a floor. She carried
bricks in, and made a stove and
two chairs. She turned the apple-
crate over to hide the broken
part, and put it in the place for
a table. She put the cups on the

table and the pan on the stove.

Penny was still sitting in
the tree.

'I think that looks nice,' said
Sarah. She said it to herself, but
loudly, in case Penny wanted to
come down and look. 'But there
ought to be flowers.' She went to
the geraniums under her bedroom
window, and picked some flowers.
She put them in a cup on the table.

Penny stared away at the
back yards.

'It's nearly dinner-time,' said
Sarah, to herself but loudly. 'Dad
will be home soon.' She waited for
a bit, but nothing happened.

This was a very bad fight, and
Penny was stuck in it.

Sarah went slowly across the
yard to the proper house. She
thought maybe her mother could
sort things out.

Mrs Bell was in the kitchen.
She said, 'You're in early. Has
Penny gone home?'

'No,' said Sarah, not looking

at anything.

'Where is she, then?'

'In the sugar-gum tree,' said Sarah.

Mrs Bell dropped a potato. 'Sarah, that tree isn't safe. You've both been told that the branches often break.'

'I know,' said Sarah. 'She won't come down.'

'Oh, Sarah, not another fight!' Mrs Bell dried her hands. 'You come with me, young lady.' She marched out to the sugar-gum tree, with Sarah trailing behind.

'Penny!' called Mrs Bell. 'Be careful of that tree, dear! Its branches break quite easily. You'd better come down now, anyway. It's nearly dinner-time.'

Penny's face got red again.

'Sarah's got to say sorry. She
called me a . . .'

'A gloop,' said Sarah in a small
voice.

'She's got to say sorry,' called
Penny, hugging the tree's trunk
in case the branch broke.

'SARAH,' said Mrs Bell sternly.

'I'm sorry,' whispered Sarah,
though she knew it wasn't fair.

'Say it louder. She's right up
the tree.'

Sarah put her head back and
shouted, 'I'M SORRY!' Then she

added, just moving her lips and
making no sound, 'That Penny
May is such a gloop.'

'She said it again!' shouted Penny. 'I saw her! She called me it again!'

'Sarah,' said Mrs Bell, 'go to your room and stay there. Penny May, I'm going to ring up your mother. She'll be home from work by now.'

Sarah slumped off to her bedroom.

Three

Sarah flopped down on her bed. She could hear Mrs Bell ringing up Mrs May. Sitting on the bed, she stared glumly out of her window. There was the quilt-house, still a bit crooked. There was Penny, so high in the sugar-gum tree that she looked small. Now her face wasn't red; it was

glum, like Sarah's, and she clung

tight to the tree.

Sarah gave her a little wave;

they were both in the same

trouble. And it must be bad for

Penny, high up in the Bells' tree
with her mother coming.

The car drove into the shed:
now Dad was home. He came into
the yard, and stopped to look at
the quilt-house, shaking his head.

He picked up his hammer and put it away. Then he went inside. He hadn't looked up into the tree.

Sarah waited. Mum and Dad were talking in the kitchen. After a while, Dad came out again.

'Hi, there!' he called into the sugar-gum. 'Are you going to stay and have dinner with Sarah?'

Penny shook her head. Her mouth was tight shut. Sarah saw that Penny couldn't talk now, even if she tried.

'It's not very nice,' called Mr Bell, 'spending the night in a tree. What if you go to sleep? Will you fall?'

Penny looked as if she might cry.

'Don't you want to get down before your mother comes?' called Mr Bell. 'We can all have a Coke while we wait.'

Penny shook her head again. Mr Bell came over to look at the geraniums. Then he looked through the window, at Sarah.

'You know you're a brat, don't you?' he said in a cross voice. 'It's time you got some sense.'

It wasn't fair, but Sarah didn't
tell him; now she couldn't talk,
either. She only looked at him,
and he went inside.

The front door-bell rang, and

the house was full of voices: both
Mr and Mrs May had come. There
was loud talking for a while, and
suddenly all the grown-ups spilt
out of the back door into the yard.

'Penny!' cried Mrs May. 'You come
down out of that tree this very
minute, do you hear?'

'And stay close to the trunk!'
called Mr May.

Penny stared at all the people.
Then she screwed up her mouth
and shut her eyes.

Mrs Bell called to her, coaxing.
'Penny, dear, I promise nobody is
going to be cross. Just come down
while it's still daylight, and before

you fall. Sarah is going to say
she's sorry.'

Penny clung to the tree and
stared away over all the back yards.

'I know what it is,' said Mrs May.
'The child is badly frightened.
Penny, dear, can you hear me?
Don't be scared, we're all here to
help. Just come down a little bit,
if you can; just one branch for now.'

Penny shut her eyes and
scrunched herself tighter to the tree.

'If you can't, never mind,' called

Mrs May quickly. 'Just hang on and keep still. Dad will call the Fire Brigade.'

Sarah gasped. The Fire Brigade! Oh, no!

'NO!' shouted Penny furiously, and shut her mouth tight. Her face was very red.

Sarah felt sick with worry.

'For goodness sake!' called Mrs May. 'What are we to do, then? You know we can't leave you in a tree all night.'

Penny kept her mouth shut.
For a minute the grown-ups
talked softly to each other. Then
Mr May went inside to call the
Fire Brigade. All the grown-ups
stood gazing into the tree.

Soon, from a long way off, came
the howling of a siren.

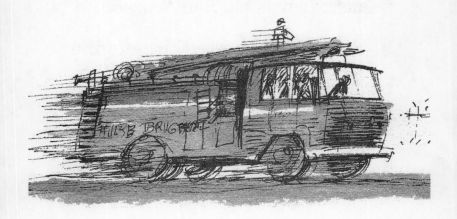

Four

The siren came nearer. Penny
wound her arms and legs harder
round the tree. Sarah felt dreadful.

The wailing noise came nearer,
nearer; it was the loudest sound
in the world. The red fire-engine
rushed howling round the corner.
It stopped outside the Bells'
back fence.

There were four firemen. They
talked in loud, kind voices to the
grown-ups and to Penny. They put

up a ladder, right over the

back fence and into the sugar-

gum tree.

One man came climbing along

the ladder. He kept talking

loudly and kindly to Penny. He
told her it was all right, she was
quite safe, he was coming; and

he told her he had a little
girl of his own, about her size.

Penny kept her eyes and
mouth tight shut. She gripped
the tree with her arms and
legs and clung like a koala. The
fireman couldn't pull her off.

'That's a good, sensible girl,' he said, 'holding on so tight. But I've got you safe; you can let go now.'

Penny didn't let go. She clung like a koala. The fireman talked and pulled for a long time. At last he gave in, and went back along the ladder. He told Mr May he was afraid of breaking the tree.

Everyone was worried. Mrs May was crying. All the firemen talked to Mr May and Mr Bell. They said something about a net.

'What for?' said Penny's
fireman. 'She's not going to fall.'

The men took the ladder
down, and Mr Bell herded
everyone into the house.

They went on talking in a
worried way. It was beginning to
get dark.

Sarah pushed her window
wide open. She put her chair
near it, climbed over the sill,

jumped down
into the
geraniums,
and ran very
fast to the
sugar-
gum tree.

'Quick, Penny!' she shouted.

'Now! This way, quick!'

Penny came climbing and
tumbling out of the tree.

Five

Penny reached the lowest
branch and fell on to Sarah. They
scrambled up and ran to the
window. The sill was high, but they
jumped and wriggled and pulled
themselves up. They had to.

At last they were standing in
Sarah's room, staring at each other.
They still couldn't believe it.

The Fire Brigade!

'What now?' said Penny in
a tight, hard voice.

Sarah didn't know what now, but
she knew it had to be fast or her
mother would be here. She said,
'We'll just get into bed, and serve

them right. Here – pyjamas –

hurry up! Mum's sure to come.'

Quickly they put on pyjamas

and climbed into Sarah's bed.

There were footsteps coming

down the hall. Sarah and Penny lay down and shut their eyes. They had just fitted themselves together when the door opened, and Mrs Bell switched on the light.

She didn't say a word. She just looked for a while and went away.

Sarah and Penny stayed as they were. They didn't know what else to do.

Then there were loud, grown-up voices saying things like *'What?'* and *'Never!'* and *'Can't be!'*

Someone – it might have been

Penny's fireman – said, '*Well, I'll*

be a monkey's uncle!' A lot of feet

came shuffling down the hall.

Sarah and Penny lay still. They
could tell that all the people were
crowding in the doorway, looking
at them.

'Kids,' said a fireman. 'Can't
beat 'em, can you?'

'I might,' said Mr Bell, but he
didn't sound cross. He sounded

very tired.

'I owe you chaps something for your trouble,' said Mr May. He sounded tired too. The firemen made soft, rumbling noises, and shuffled away down the hall after Mr May.

Sarah and Penny opened their eyes. Mr and Mrs Bell and Mrs May were still there. They all looked tired.

'Penny's staying the night,' said Sarah. 'Aren't you, Penny?'

'Umph,' grunted Penny. She

still couldn't talk much.

'Is she?' said Mrs Bell.

'I thought you'd had a fight.'

'It couldn't be helped,' said Sarah. 'It was *our* fight.'

'Fair enough,' said Mr Bell, 'and it's *our* sugar-gum tree. And the next person who climbs it is going to get well and truly spanked.'

'Twice,' added Mrs May.

'Three times,' said Mr May coming back.

'That's fair enough too,' said Mrs Bell, 'but I promised Penny no one would be cross if she came down. Do you think this time we might just feed them and shut them up in Sarah's room till morning?'

'Well . . .' said Mrs and Mr May, thinking it over.

Sarah and Penny stayed in bed. It seemed safest, and they were tired too.

Six

In the end, Mr and Mrs May
went home and Penny stayed
with Sarah. They were still in bed,
and Mrs Bell brought them dinner
on a tray. It was hard to manage,
with two people in one bed.

'You're tipping it up!' cried
Sarah when Penny moved
her legs.

'Stop knocking my elbow, Sarah,'
growled Penny.

Later, when the light was out,
they lay fitted together and
thought about things. Sarah was
nearly asleep when Penny jerked
a bit and woke her up.

'Do you have to joggle?' said

Sarah, sleepy. 'What's up?'

'The . . . the Fire Brigade!'

whispered Penny, and pulled the blanket over her head and shook with giggles.

Sarah was surprised and glad, so she started giggling too. 'I'll be a monkey's uncle!' she whispered, and they giggled about that. They went on giggling till they fell asleep.

Seven

In the morning, after breakfast, Penny went home. Sarah went with her to the gate.

'I'll bring my teaset,' said Penny.

'Good,' said Sarah. She climbed on the gate to watch Penny walk away down the pavement.

When Penny was nearly at the

corner, Sarah leaned out from
the gate and shouted, 'Penny!'

Penny stopped and turned back.

'I'm sorry . . .'

'Oh, no!' cried Penny, and
started to run.

'. . . THAT PENNY MAY IS SUCH A GLOOP!' shouted Sarah as fast as she could.

But Penny had turned the corner just in time.

From Patricia Wrightson

I wrote *The Sugar-Gum Tree* a long time ago
as a picture book, but it wasn't right for the
big, colourful kind. I put it away.

Much later I met David Cox. He read the story,
liked it, and wanted to illustrate it, so we
talked to Puffin. That was the first time David
and I worked together, and since then he has
worked on all my *Aussie Bites*. We seem to like
the same lively sort of character.

From David Cox

I like the people in *The Sugar-Gum Tree*.
When the people are so different from one
another, it is easier, somehow, to see them in
my mind. I added just one more, which
is the dog. We do not know his name; he is just
there, always watching. All the arguments
and drama must seem puzzling to him.
Humans are a funny lot, and, come to think
of it, that is what the story is all about.

PUFFIN BOOKS

Aussie Bites

the water-dragons

Sam, Lin and Jerry all had
water-dragons, who lived in
the drain near their homes.
Now the Council was going to
clean up the drain.

What would happen to the
water-dragons?

Aussie Bites

the Water dragons

Patricia Wrightson
illustrated by David Cox

Puffin Books

One

There was a big, deep drain behind
Mann Street. It used to be a boggy
creek before the town grew over it,
but now it was a concrete drain.
Weeds grew near it, and slimy
weeds in the cracks of the concrete.
Paper and rubbish were washed
into it. There was a dark tunnel
where it ran under Bent Street,
and a small bridge for walking
across it.

Sam lived in Mann Street, and the drain was just behind his back fence. Lin lived in Burke Street; she hardly ever saw Mann Street, but her back garden ran down to the drain, the same as Sam's did. Jerry lived in Skinners Lane, with the

2

drain running along his side fence.

Sam and Lin and Jerry went to
the same school. They were not
good friends or bad friends; they
were just the ones who lived near
the drain. That's why they all had
tame lizards.

3

The lizards were water-dragons. They were big, with wide, flat bodies shaped like great, broad leaves. Their tails were thin like whips, and the dragons could move as fast as a whip.

If they were frightened, they
lifted their heads and opened
their mouths very wide. Then you
could see their pink tongues, and
a long row of small, flat teeth.
With the spiky bristles under
their chins, they looked fierce;
but really they were friendly and
a little bit shy.

The dragons were partly tame, but still partly wild. They did not live in cages; they were good at looking after themselves. Sam would hear his dragon rustling among ferns in the front garden.

Lin's liked to lie in the sun
behind her dad's compost heap.

Jerry's often dozed under the
back steps.

But all of them went off to secret
places of their own, and Jerry's dad
said those would be in the drain.

'They're water-dragons,' he said. 'It's the only water handy.'

'Yuk!' said Jerry, pretending to choke. 'That slimy stuff!' But he told Sam and Lin about it when he happened to see them. Jerry's mum and dad used to live on a farm. Now his dad worked for the Council but he still knew a lot about animals. Jerry didn't mind passing it on.

Two

Jerry called his water-dragon
Flower. This was partly because,
the first time they met, she got a

fright. When her big mouth gaped open there were chewed-up flowers in it. Partly it was because Flower was the name of a nice, friendly cow they used to have on the farm.

Jerry hardly ever picked up his dragon; his dad said she didn't like it. But she liked him to feed her, and to hold her while he rubbed a special place under her chin. That made her nod stiffly, like a wooden lizard.

Lin called her dragon Zeb. That was short for Zebra, because she saw faint, blotchy stripes on his

yellow–grey skin. They used to meet behind the compost heap, even before they made friends. Now Zeb came for breakfast every morning.

Lin would bang his feeding-tin with a spoon. Zeb would come along the path in little runs, short and fast. He would come quite near and eat from the tin: bits of salad and fruit, some moths that Lin had caught, perhaps a worm or two from the garden.

Sometimes he even took food from Lin's hand. That was exciting,

and it was enough. She didn't want
him any tamer; it was like having a
friend. She didn't want to carry
him, or sit him on her shoulder. Not
with those long, twisty claws.

Sam called his dragon Dinosaur:
Dino for short. Every day, after
school, he would cut some meat
into very small pieces and look for
Dino among the ferns. He would
lift the lizard to his shoulder and
it would sit there. It would make
little, sudden grabs, taking pieces
of meat from his fingers. Then he
would lift it down, and it would

whisk away through the ferns to
one of its secret places.

'He's no trouble at all, only for
feeding,' Sam declared at school.
'Other times I hardly see him.' He
was skiting to some smaller boys at
lunch in the shelter-shed; he knew

17

none of them had a water-dragon.

Lin was having lunch in the
shelter-shed too. 'It's only in winter
you don't see them,' she told the
smaller boys. 'And by spring they're
dreadfully hungry. Zeb's just
starving! I can't find enough clover

and insects and stuff.'

Sam frowned. He didn't like to
have another dragon-keeper cutting
in. 'You should give him meat, then,'
he said sternly. 'He can find insects
and stuff for himself, easy. He has
to *catch* meat.'

'Not cow, he doesn't,' called Jerry,
cutting in too. He was eating his
lunch on the other side of the shed.
'I bet no one ever saw a water-
dragon eating a cow, like what you
feed Dino. Dad says Flower knows
what's good for her, and *she* likes

20

insects and eggs and green stuff.
Dad says insects are meat.'

Now there were two people
putting Sam right. His voice grew
louder. 'I saw that Flower! I was
down at the drain. I looked over
your fence.'

'It must've been near five,' said
Jerry, not loudly at all. 'She'd be
coming for her dinner.'

'She's not grown enough, I can
tell you that! Dino's a lot bigger.
Yours wants more meat.'

Jerry glared. 'Who says she's
not grown enough? Dino's fat.

He's having a heart attack soon, from all that meat.'

Sam stood up taller to look down at Jerry. He was a year ahead. 'I'm just telling you, that's all. I've seen this Zeb, too. He's not a proper colour – all yellow-looking, not grey. He wants more meat.'

Lin snorted. She was in the same year as Sam and just as tall. She said, 'Nobody asked you, Sam Ford. If you want to see my water-dragon you can come round and ask! You don't have to sneak about looking over fences.'

'You ought to be glad,' Sam shouted. 'Don't you want to know if your dragons are sick? Don't you care if they're too small? And the wrong colour?'

Jerry growled at him: 'Look, you:

my dad grew up in the bush and he knows about water-dragons. So you can stuff it.'

It was nearly a fight, right there in the shelter-shed having lunch. But Sam and Lin and Jerry didn't

know each other well enough to fight. They just stopped talking; and after that they kept away from each other.

Three

At home, they told their water-dragons about it.

'You look magic,' said Lin to Zeb.

'Maybe you were a bit pale in winter, but your new skin's terrific.'

Zeb snatched a bit of apple from her fingers, and veiled his eyes while he chewed.

'There, then,' said Lin. 'You don't want meat, do you?'

Zeb snatched another bit of apple. You could tell he loved apple better than anything.

*

'You'll show them,' said Sam. He felt shivery with Dino's claws gripping his shoulder, but he never told anyone that. He said, 'You could lick both those others. Have some more meat.'

Dino made a sudden grab, and chewed and swallowed.

'That's it,' said Sam. 'Get big and strong.'

Dino spread his legs and gripped with his claws. You could see he thought meat was best for anyone.

*

'Come on, then,' said Jerry.

He reached under the steps to lift Flower out, and rubbed the place under her chin. She jerked her head up and down like a clockwork toy.

Jerry gave her a dish of chopped
lettuce with hard-boiled egg and
garden-worms.

'If you're still hungry after that,'
he said, 'we'll go and find a cow.'

Flower ate her meal with slow
enjoyment and went back under the

steps. She was turning her back on the cow.

*

But at school next week, Jerry went looking for Sam and Lin. There was something he had to tell them.

He waited for them after school, down at the gate. There was an old fig tree and a seat, but none of them sat down. They just stood there, not saying much because last time there was nearly a fight.

'It's the Council,' said Jerry at last.

'Where your dad works,' said Lin, sniffing.

'It's always your dad,' said Sam.

'You don't have to listen.'

Lin said, 'Go on.'

'They're going to clean up the drain,' said Jerry. 'There'll be back hoes, and wire brushes, and poison for weeds. Dad says I should shut Flower up in a box.'

'Dino can't be shut in a box!' said Sam roundly.

'Suit yourself. It's only one day. I don't want Flower chopped up or poisoned.'

'Zeb won't go near the drain!' cried Lin. 'Not with back hoes and wire brushes and a lot of men!' She wasn't even sure if she *could* catch Zeb.

'He's a water-dragon,' snapped Jerry. 'He goes to water. But it's your funeral.'

Sam and Lin stood frowning. Jerry shrugged and turned to the gate. Lin asked, 'When do they start?'

'Monday,' Jerry told her.

'The fruit-shop has big, strong boxes,' said Sam.

They all went off through the gate, not saying any more.

Lin didn't want to talk to the others; she could look after her own dragon, thank you — but she needed time to think about it. Zeb was quite big. She had never even thought of catching him. He looked heavy, and he might not be as tame as Dino or Flower. He might hate being caught so much that he'd run off and never come back.

Four

In the next few days Lin didn't try
to catch Zeb. She stroked him a lot:
he felt rough and dry, not soft like a

skink. He didn't mind being
stroked. He just went on eating.

Sam was right about the fruit-
shop. The man gave her a strong,
deep box with a good lid. It even
had air-holes; they were big, but
not so big that Zeb might get out.
Lin put the box near the daisy-
bushes in the garden. She went to
the kitchen to find an old dish.

'Can I have this one, Mum? It's
all cracked.'

Her mother was putting the
groceries away. She looked up with
a packet of flour in her hand. 'Yes,

all right. Put it in the garbage
when you've finished with it, like a
good girl.'

Lin filled the dish with water
and stood it in Zeb's box. It stood
level on the cardboard floor. She
put some dead fern-leaves in the

box for a nest. On Sunday morning
she called Zeb to the daisy-bushes
for his feed.

He squatted and slowly munched
a worm. Lin suddenly whipped him
up in one hand, the feeding-tin in
the other, popped them into the box

and pushed the lid on as fast as she could. Then she waited to see what would happen.

Nothing happened. The box did not rock or wobble as if Zeb were fighting to get out. There was no loud *zap!* from his lashing tail; nothing but little scraping sounds as he went on eating.

Lin could hardly believe it. Now she need only worry about having to take the lid off for his next feed.

All morning she kept creeping back to the daisy-bushes. The box was always quiet and peaceful and safe. It was when she went back after lunch that she saw Sam.

He was clinging to the back fence, looking over; he must have climbed up from the drain. He hung on with one arm and waved with the other. Lin thought he was trying to see Zeb again. She started down to the fence, to tell him Zeb was shut in the box. But as she came near he called out to her.

'You didn't see Dino, did you?'

Lin was astonished. 'No, why? What's wrong?'

Sam tried to shrug and almost

fell. 'Nothing, only I have to catch him. His box is ready. It's getting late.'

'Isn't he there?'

'No,' said Sam. He looked worried. 'Never came for his feed. I've got it here.' He groped in his pocket and fell off the fence.

Five

Jerry came later, when the sun was setting. He came through the front gate, round to the back garden. He

had a paper shopping bag. He
called to Lin, 'Have you seen
Flower?'

'Of course not,' said Lin. She had
never seen Flower, or Dino either.
She didn't play with dragons like
kittens; she had never even caught
her own Zeb until now. It was Lin
who should be upset and needing
help – not Sam and Jerry, who
handled their dragons every day.
'What's up?' she asked crossly.

'How do I know?' said Jerry, just
as crossly. 'She's not here, that's all.
Just when I need her, she's not here.'

'Why come asking me?'

'*I* don't know. I can't *find* her, can I? I just thought she might be friends with yours, or mating or something. You've got to look *somewhere*.'

There was a shout from the back fence. It was Sam again. He came tumbling over the fence.

'What does *he* want?' Jerry demanded.

'Dino's lost. I told him it's not here.'

Sam came running up the yard calling, 'Hey! Hey, Jerry! Have you seen Dino?'

47

'No, I haven't,' growled Jerry.
'Have you seen Flower?' They all
stood frowning.

At that moment there came
a bloggy sort of noise from the
daisy-bushes.

'What's that?' cried Lin. Had
some horrible dragon-eater taken
Dino and Flower? And had it come
back now for Zeb? She took two
quick steps towards the big, round
daisy-bushes. Their leaves stirred,
and a water-dragon's head looked
out. Lin and Sam and Jerry all
cried out together.

'Zeb!'

'Dino!'

'Flower!'

The water-dragon made a little rush from the daisy-bushes to the path.

'You've got out of your box!' cried Lin.

'How did you get here?' cried Sam.

'Where have you been?' cried Jerry.

They all stopped staring at the water-dragon and began to stare at each other.

Six

'It's not true!' cried Lin. 'That's Zeb! It's not Dino and it's not Flower. It's Zeb.'

'How do you know?' Jerry demanded.

'Of course I know!' cried Lin. 'I know Zeb! He came when I called him. He's always the same. He's the one I shut in the box, and he's been there all the time!'

'He's still there, then,' said Sam.

He picked up the dragon. 'Have a look. Because this is Dino.'

'In a pig's ear,' growled Jerry. 'It's Flower.'

But Lin had rushed away into the daisy-bushes. 'He's not there!' she called. 'His water-dish leaked.

The box is all soggy and there's a big hole. It *is* Zeb. He's got out.'

The boys didn't answer. They were watching the water-dragon. It was sitting on Sam's shoulder and eating pieces of meat. 'Good boy, Dino,' crooned Sam. He groped in his pocket for more meat.

Jerry clenched his hands. 'All right,' he said. 'Now watch this.' He took the dragon off Sam's shoulder and held it against his chest. Lin came back looking worried, and watched too.

Jerry rubbed the place under the

dragon's chin. Its head bobbed up and down stiffly, like a wooden puppet. 'Good girl, Flower,' crooned Jerry. 'You don't want to be stuffed with bits of cow, do you?'

'It's *not* Flower!' cried Lin. 'And it's not Dino! He came when I called him! He took food out of my hand! He's called Zeb because of his stripes – you can see them!'

'Stripes?' said Sam. 'Not Dino. More like blotches, see? If Zeb's got stripes he's not this one. This is Dino.'

'You said Dino was a different

colour! Grey, you said! And bigger!'

Sam looked at the dragon and grinned. 'Anyone can see he's bigger. A lot bigger.'

Lin gazed at the dragon that Jerry was holding. 'I don't care what you say,' she said helplessly. 'It's Zeb.'

'I reckon,' said Jerry, making the dragon nod its head again. 'I reckon it's Zeb. And I reckon it's Dino. And I know for sure it's Flower.'

Sam snorted. 'Talk sense.'

'I reckon it's sense,' said Jerry. 'This one comes when Lin calls it.

And it sits on your shoulder. And it
nods when I scratch it. It never said
where it lived, and it never said it
was Dino or Zeb or Flower. That's
only what we said. *It* just went on
around its own place, making
friends and dropping in for a meal.
We did the rest.'

'You mean . . .' said Lin, 'it's only
one dragon . . . and we don't really
have any.' She knew it was true, but
it made her sad.

Jerry shook his head. 'We've got
what we had before, can't you see?
What's changed?'

Lin and Sam thought about it.

'Is it Flower or Dino, then?' Sam demanded. 'Girl or boy? It's got to be one.'

Jerry shrugged. 'What's the difference? Is it grey or yellow? Big or little? Stripy or blotched?

Who cares?'

Lin said, 'When you've got
friends, they have other friends too.
And their own house and
everything . . . At least we can't
fight any more about which is
biggest, or what they all eat . . .'

'Want to bet?' said Jerry. 'It'll be
different for one day, while they
clean the drain. Then it'll go back
the way it was. Dad made me a
proper box for Flower, so what if I
put her in?'

The others nodded. Jerry slid the
dragon into the shopping bag.

'Hang on,' said Sam, groping in his pocket. 'You'll need his meat for tomorrow.' Lin and Jerry laughed, and in a minute Sam laughed too.

They could see that from now on they would just have to be friends.

From Patricia Wrightson

There are often lizards around our house, sometimes tiny ones inside it. We catch a glimpse of the Bathroom Skink, the Laundry Skink, the Verandah Skink. Once a goanna clung to a fly-screen for an hour. One year it was hard to cut the grass because of all the water-dragons in the yard.

Our dogs are not allowed to chase them. My dog Daisy had a short cut from the back yard to the front, going between the house and the tank; but sometimes a water-dragon sat there. Then Daisy would growl crossly, back out and go the long way round. We got to know the water-dragons well that year.

From David Cox

For a while we had a water-dragon visit us. It liked to lie on top of a wall and take the sun. We live near the top of Highgate Hill and usually there is not much water lying about, so after a while it went away.

When I came to illustrate *The Water-Dragons*, I looked at lots of pictures of water-dragons, but what helped me the most was the memory of the one who came to visit.

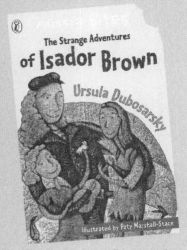

Isador carries six things in his
satchel on his travels, one of
which is a secret until nearly the
end of the story.

Holly dreams of life as a princess
on a tropical island. Suddenly
Xavier appears – to make it all
come true . . .

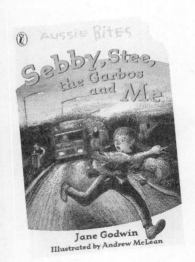

Garbos, Christmas beer and
a duck. That's when the
adventure begins . . .

Jammy and Red think Drong
Drong Island is their special place.
When they discover two girls on
their island, the battle is on!

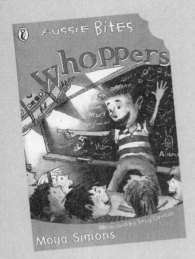

Mark swears he's a martian.
But is he telling the truth – or is
it another *whopper*?

Brian knows the removalists
are taking away the
wrong house.

Snag is thin and weedy, and he
faints at the sight of blood.
Now he's been sent to gladiator
school. It's either fight or die.

Austin finds a gold nugget
right in the middle of the
footy field.

A horrible holiday? You bet!
A car full of smelly nappies,
a constipated dog . . . Can
anything else go wrong?

Everyone is always telling Alice
to hurry up. Until one day when
Alice is first for a change . . .

Merry dreams of being a
ballerina. And nothing is
going to stop her . . .

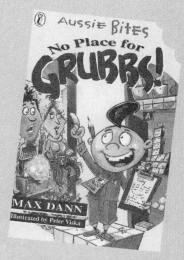

Charles Grubb is very tidy. But
his parents are real grubs. So
Charles decides to clean them up.

Come exploring at

www.penguin.com.au

and

www.puffin.com.au

for

Author and illustrator profiles

Book extracts

Reviews

Competitions

Activities, games and puzzles

Advice for budding authors

Tips for parents

Teacher resources